Mucumber McGee

AND THE
HALF-EATEN HOT DOG

written and illustrated by

PATRICK LOEHR

Katherine Tegen Books
An Imprint of HarperCollins Publishers

Mucumber McGee and the Half-Eaten Hot Dog
Copyright © 2007 by Patrick Loehr
Manufactured in China.

Library of Congress Cataloging-in-Publication Data is available.
ISBN-10: 0-06-082327-5 (trade bdg.) — ISBN-13: 978-0-06-082327-6 (trade bdg.)
ISBN-10: 0-06-082328-3 (lib. bdg.) — ISBN-13: 978-0-06-082328-3 (lib. bdg.)

Design by Martha Rago
1 2 3 4 5 6 7 8 9 10 ❖ First Edition

For Christy, Mom, and the Grandmas

IN A RAINY OLD village
down by the sea,
lived a young boy
named Mucumber McGee.

His stomach was empty
and his hunger was great,
for it had been quite a while
since Mucumber last ate.

He had slept right through dinner
and forgot about lunch,
and there was nothing for breakfast
on which he could munch.

He scoured the pantry
at the end of the hall.
He looked through the cupboards,
he looked through them all.

To the icebox he went
with great hope for a snack,
where he found one last hot dog
tucked in the back.

Through his lips, past his tongue,
down his throat to his tummy,
he had swallowed half the wiener
when his sister came running.

"Oh, Mucumber, Mucumber,
what is it you are doing?
What is it you are holding?
What is it you are chewing?"

"Is that a hot dog you are holding?
Is that a hot dog that I saw?
Is that a hot dog you are chewing?
And are you eating it RAW?"

———— ❦ ————

"Don't you know, Mucumber,
that hot dogs are made of meat?
And fleshy meat that is not cooked
is deadly bad to eat!"

———— ❦ ————

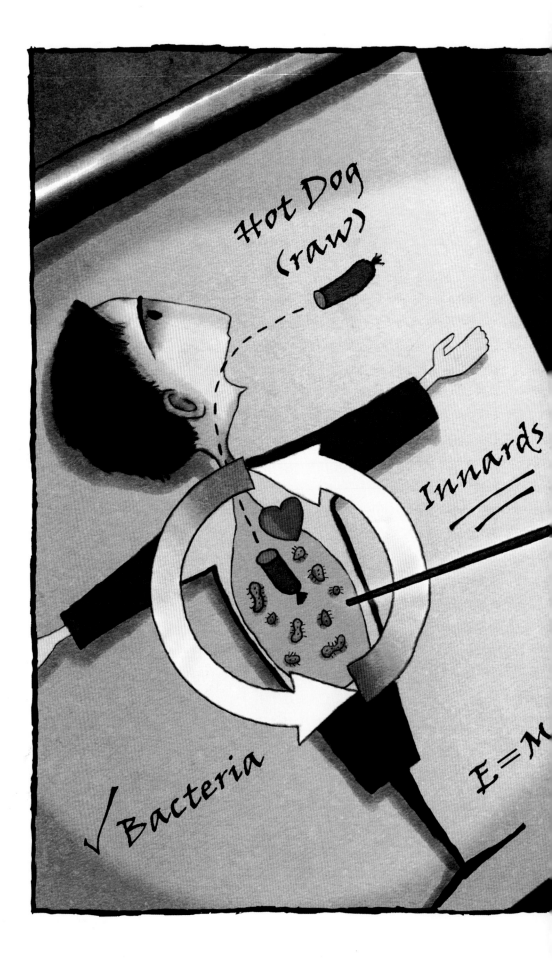

"You'll be sickened, you'll be paralyzed,
you'll be ill enough to cry.
Your insides will turn upside down!
It's reported you might die."

"DIE?" said Mucumber.
"Oh my goodness golly gee.
I was simply hungry—
I was as hungry as can be."

Then his stomach began to ache;
it growled and turned and spun.
"This is it," Mucumber thought.
"The dying has begun."

And so upstairs he ran,
with teardrops in his eyes.
"I guess I'll lie down on the bed,
and then I'll wait to die."

Mucumber gently put his head down
on his favorite pillow,
and sadly gazed out toward the old
and fragile weeping willow.

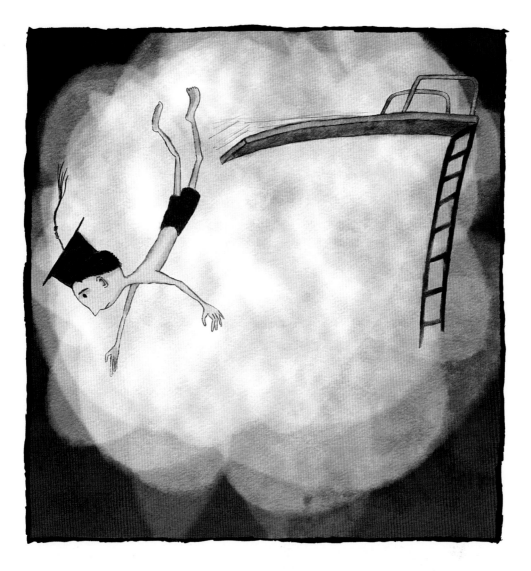

He would miss so many things in life
if he were not alive.
Like his graduation.
Like the high dive.

Just as the teardrops
were starting to pour,
in came his mother
through the bedroom door.

"Mucumber? Mucumber?
Why are you distressed?
Your eyes are all teary;
your hair is a mess."

"Oh, Mother, I'm sorry
but my life is through.
I did something awful that
I did not mean to do.

I ate a cold wiener
without cooking it first.
And now the bacteria
will cause me to burst!"

His mother leaned over
and kissed his head gently.
She looked in his eyes
and said quite intently,

"Sweet Mucumber, don't worry.
If you'd only looked,
the package says clearly:
Hot dogs are precooked!"

"PRECOOKED!" said Mucumber.
"Glory be! Whoop-de-do!
So I'm not going to die?
So my life isn't through?"

"Good gracious," said Mother.
"You're silly as a clam.
Now come to the kitchen,
where I've cooked you a ham.

And I've made you a plum cake . . .
and a salad of greens . . .
and a bushel of berries . . .
and a bucket of beans."

And all was then well
in that house by the sea.
So children, please listen,
now listen to me.

The next time your stomach
is growling and empty,
don't dig in the fridge
or the cupboards or pantry . . .

Don't listen to others,
like sisters or brothers.
Next time you are hungry . . .

just go ask your mothers.